JAKO
BOOKS

Acclaim for Modeste Downes

First (2004) recipient of the George Odlum Award for Creative Artists

Winner of the 2005 M&C main prize for literature

Winner of the 2013 CDF National Arts Award for poetry

Appointed to the St. Lucia Writers' Forum September 2015 Laureate's Chair

Also by Modeste Downes

Phases (poetry, 2005)
Theatre of the Mind (poetry, 2012)

A LESSON ON WINGS

Modeste Downes

JAKO BOOKS

New York, London, Toronto, Vieux Fort

Published in the United States by Jako Books, a division of Jako Productions.

First Jako Books Edition, February 2019
www.jakoproductions.com

LCCN: 2019931092
ISBN: 978-0-9704432-9-8

Printed in the United States of America

I am immensely indebted to Anderson Reynolds, Brian Francis, the National Farmers & General Workers Cooperative Credit Union, Alwyn St. Omer, Dawn French, Jolien Harmsen, and Victor Marquis for their support and encouragement.

Table of Contents

A LESSON
ON
WINGS

This Mangrove

This mangrove that you view
this dejected, rejected child
clad routinely in green fatigues
feet and fingers barnacled
rooted in silent, brackish water
hemline adjusting by unseen hands
dancing to the tide's soft rhythm
after each redundant wave
lands with clamour and wide gestures
frothing at the mouth, ending in nothing;

this mangrove that you view
is home too, like yours of wood and zinc
feigning comforts unattainable
yet, its head dazzling in the midday sun.

This mangrove, ostracized like a leper
is home too, if you ask the speechless ones
the shelled crabs, incubating crustaceans
the white-robed egrets that egress
with obligatory punctuality
and return, like monks to their muted cell
home again, no different than you do
to this mangrove that you view
obeying the stiff dictates of time
each day, same sun-declining hour
in practiced formation, or loose, as moved.

This mangrove that you view
that cradles the fish you'll savour tomorrow
oblivious of origin, the spawning
nestled in the protective claws of trees
whose heads alone you see bobbing, acquiescing
is life transcending the charwoman's
eking out a life from choice limbs
is saviour indeed, and giver of life.

This mangrove that you view
that you avoid like a roadside beggar
whose breath reeks of Job's festering sore
effluvium of the energy it burns
prompting your hand to defer your breathing
is busy rebuilding what you kill.

This mangrove that you view
is home too, protects lives too
and, like yours, has a right to be.

Forgotten Past

The mind, as memory
is unreliable
and often falters.

It sifts and retains
those fragments it favours
and decades later

someone will ask you
of the place you were born
something you should know—

tabula rasa.
Nothing shows on your page;
you scorn your shadow.

There's history, you know
in juvenile anecdotes
that meant nothing then

until, in despair
you search for some morsel
of that moment when

records were not stored
on computers or disks
but raw in the head.

And when the poor mind
is as porous as sponge
the devil eat your bread.

As a sufferer
I often encounter
faces from a past

whose memory, like smoke
a vapoury thing
is gone with the blast.

Lanège, Masinel
The *fijé* by the rock
Osiole's whirlpool

or ghosts by Valcin's
return to me like breath
as it should, as a rule.

But for so much more
I struggle to recall.
Like a rootless tree

my poor mind shudders.
Amnesiac in the wind
I pain for my history.

Couplets for Lent

They're at it again, this crime-stoned year—
The season of penitence and fear,

Sin gridlocked for the death of Christ.
Lucifer goads the poltergeist,

To upset the faithful at prayer,
Ducks burning incense scenting the air.

Banners the colour of sadness,
Like the priest's vestments that suppress

Gaiety and ill-timed celebration,
Stand staid as at the crucifixion.

Chants of guilt soar smooth as a floor tile:
'O come and mourn with me a while...'

Link worshippers to Gethsemane;
'Christ have mercy, have mercy on me...'

Processing to venerate holy wood,
Their ingrates at home, glued to Hollywood.

'At the cross her station keeping,
Stood his mother, Mary, weeping...'

Parody of shame, singing the blues,
Cringing at Rome's way with seditious Jews.

This year, again, *carne vale*,
A nostalgic whiff of yesterday;

Still, Ash Wednesday's ritual persists,
Single file they crawl, cold like Judas' kiss.

Covert insult of the priest's thumb—
'Mwen tann ou di ou sé on nonm?'

'By the sweat of thy brow...Ash to ash...'
Man ain't get the point, he's such an ass.
I dust my autographed Walcott:
We're just erect ash—what a thought!

Six Stanzas for Children of the Sun

The sun ascends like *banja* vines
With purpose from the break of day.
What God with burning on his mind
Commissions him, I cannot say.

Startled clouds melt to let him pass
Sometimes perforce they drop their rain.
With seeming arrogance and class
Some say the sun is rather vain.

I watch in minimizing awe
At this mysterious thing of fire
Slither along without a flaw
As it rises like a spire.

At noon, his most defiant hour
Phoebus does seem to rest awhile
And radiating all his power
As from a source at just a mile.

At evening time, predictably
Tired of trekking the curved blue sky
He drowns his light deliberately
And with a green flash, says goodbye.

Don't think I do not like the sun.
If that's your bent, you're doubly wrong.
Without his energizing gun
Nothing would grow healthy and strong.

A Lesson on Wings

A seagull circles overhead, ominously
then jets downward, swift like an arrow from a bow
touches ground, and with a limp, settles cautiously

atop a bleached stump. As if in meditation
she pensively regards the silvered sea below
then swiveling, she sweeps the landscape in slow motion.

Survey done, this analyst limps a few paces
then, like a ritual, circles the stump where she laid
and suddenly, takes flight. I thank God for such graces.

For while the limb-impaired bird has a choice of wings
enfeebled man, a gnat, without another's aid
condemned pedestrian, might be tutored by such things.

I hear the pounding of fleets for Helen by waves
against the craggy cape and shell-slapped rocks below
barrier unmoved, though battering sea may rant and rave.

Alone now, I contemplate my fragility
the common lot assigned to all—*piti kon gwo*
man's inevitable end—dark mortality.

360 Degrees

The routine of conduct of late
So vulgar, I must speculate
If we don't about-turn, and fast
We'll soon be a thing of the past.

Today's sun is so bloody hot
I'm a stew in a brown clay pot
Tight-lidded and slung in the midst
Of Soufriere's volcanical mist.

It was once canonical, I know
Of a time not that long ago
When elders had respect and place.
Now imps treat them with sheer disgrace.

Eating was near sacramental
When man was not quite animal,
Engorging all manner of shit
Scornfully stamped 'GM' on it.

From Eden, egg yolk was yellow
Like the *'Giné'* we used to grow.
Now crack a new age one, I bet
You'll declare all fowls faggots.

The trend-setters, truly simian
With altered brain, or none to scan
Just as frogs on the road are crushed
Their own shadow they treat as dust.

With material fixed on the mind
Each grabs on to what he can find:
Let the devil take the hindmost
Or starved Death—whichever comes first.

The Unfortunate Traveller

Our Nobelist bard,
in select tongue characteristic,
depicts the pathetic lot of man,
unfortunate traveller,
like an unguided missile,
he knows neither whence he came,
nor where to lay down his load.
No trophies at the end of the road:
Do not pass GO
Do not collect two hundred dollars!

Poor man, shadowed by a question mark,
his appointment with destiny,
like Damocles' sword above his head,
a death sentence decreed at first breath,
reward for Adam's adventurism,
who discovered more than Columbus,
but ended more vulnerable than a worm.

Why should a seed be envious
of a condition with no cure,
of a poison without antidote:
'to flower
to suffer
to die'?
Birth,
    growth,
        degeneration,
            death.
Ash to ash,
dust to dust. That's all?

And, utters the psalmist,
'even his thoughts perish'.

Bestial

O cloven-hoofed beast
swimming out of the swamp
in the dark of night.

Dark creature of slough
monomaniac of slime
ordained to spawn filth.

Your doomed endeavour
is hell's fecal mission
to upset the good.

Come at breakneck speed
or dive like a meteor.
Either way, you lose.

New Perspective

All around in muted phrases
is a poetry uncollated.
A font of knowledge and wisdom
each leaf that ripens and falls
each shooting star that slides out of place
each grain of sand trampled underfoot
is a parable paraphrased—
as dying, too, is life cut short
a thing that performs, being disabled
that teaches, its licence annulled.

The sea dictates its learning
to rolling pages wet with ambition.
And as stubbornly as waves come and go
all dying prefaces rebirth;
laughter has meaning only
because it knows its sister, tears.

Sometimes I wonder what I'd be
had God or the Fates been kinder
that I was a rolling brook
skipping stones, singing without cease
or a many-karat diamond
lodged deep in the bosom of earth
unfound, never to be found
never to be shaped by tool or mind
to glut maniacal desires.

Hardly a day of books on shelves
of ideas born, of things, of selves
that patience fails to intervene
to counter an obstructionist scheme.
I've come to view life differently
guardian of decades, less agile

than I pretend, even alone.
I do not claim old friendships
any more than I recall
what the garbage man has lifted.
I regret valued things I've lost
but whatever is gone, is past.
Even friendship, which is like money—
you use it because you have it.

Each death I hear intoned by waves
every funeral I hate to attend
my mouth turns bitter like sour milk
my mind trembles like a milkshake;
the arched sky unfurls a black shroud
Damocles' stinger suspending.
To the fatal swipe of the blade
I bow, like a branch at vespers;
I quake at the spading of dust
that deletes a figure once buoyant.

I'm short on sleep, deliberating
disposing of dreams in my head.
I care less for joyous living
it's in the wind, I'll soon be dead.
But though I'm earth like other men
I have the endurance of ten.

Words of Wisdom

Stranger things have happened
Than drug babes in a womb
Worse things couldn't happen
Than beauty in a tomb

Wise men never falter
Not even for a heart
But a heart may shatter
When fluttered by a tart

Adam was a sinner
Who slipped and slid on pride
Eve was even meaner
No wonder both did hide

Trials and misfortune
Are seldom without friend
Good men know their sad croon
Careening round a bend

Many men have spoken
But mostly foolish thoughts
If wisdom's but a token
Let foolish men draw lots.

Numbering His Days

For God so dearly loved the world,
Being complete—so I am told,
He deemed it never to grow old.

The first man, Adam, and his mate,
Birds, fish and all things animate,
Would grow but not degenerate.

But man would not be engineered
To walk the way that God desired—
He dared to suit himself instead.

Smart man, he read books and got wise,
Imbibed more wickedness and vice
And soon, with God he severed ties.

Inventive man brewed alcohol,
Designed himself another fall,
Pivoting in his own pitfall.

More wayward as the days went by,
Forgetting whence he came, and why,
He blindly coursed the way to die.

And God, being mighty tolerant,
Saw all, but lifted not a hand;
But I, as God, would take a stand.

Mean time and man, they strolled along,
God's plan going seemingly wrong,
And man feeling strong like King Kong.

One day he found a looking glass,
And glimpsed his features as he passed,
He paused to wonder why, at last:

His skin wrinkled, his hair was gray,
His strength waned at the end of day,
Shorter his days, the Scriptures say.

Thus, all the beauty of creation
Suffers the common condition:
Ageing, dying—no exemption.

Before and After

I saw her today, a sudden gust of wind.
A wiry, deep-fried twig of a woman,
Once, by the grace of generous circumstance—
When her medaling petals had not been so twisted,
Or perhaps the landscape was penciled more lightly,
And your retina reflected far less than its range—
She outperformed the golden orb that eats its shadow,
A too seasoned recipe that teased the taste buds.

As she traipsed past prying eyes, feigning urgency,
Some branches of the jocose bougainvillea
Curtsied, as though it meant anything to them,
As they, more than any, secure in their knowledge
Of her, could decode what lay behind the façade.

Instinctively, I fixed on the rearview instead.

Times Not Good for Verse

So many failed lyrics in my closet,
Masterpieces that refuse to be born,
Blue lines stroking the face of innocent
White sheets that lie, crisp, waiting for stillborns,
Impotent poet doubling as midwife.

So many distractions in the changing air,
Of a time when green leaves shudder and fall,
So pervasive and constant the fear and
Uncertainty that colours things everywhere.

No more the absoluteness of seasons,
Of the changing face of clouds before rain,
Of infants maturing into knowing,
Before their crawling diapers absorb guilt.

Nature abhors a vacuum, it is said.
Thus, with the emptiness that abounds,
Art capitulates for lack of audience,
Creativity either a stillborn,
Or with luck, survives, a goose-fleshed midget.

So many failed lyrics in my closet.

Masking

After listening, halfheartedly,
to the designer televangelist
playing an angry Moses,
his audience—not congregation—
higher on entertainment than inspiration,
I fancied his theme, unwittingly
meat well seasoned for my next poem:
the obsession with masks.

A Pavlovian or Freudian trait,
a learned vice reverberating
the dirge of epochal shame,
to falsify the mirror face of truth.
We mount this black robed enigma
because the light is too honest.
Unwittingly a black man's patent,
baggage we carry from the old plantation,
trademark of the hoarder of skeletons,
regression to the pre-Cambrian.

We sanitize carnival and call it art.
Without precedent or history,
we clown about with Halloween.
Women overcoat their natural sheen
and overdose on mascara.
'How're you doing?'
We say, 'Fine', when we're anything but.
Oh, the lengths we go for camouflage!

So steeped are we in vain deceit,
we cede to traffickers of the dark,
the polished highway we craved,
reverting to long forgotten tracks.
We exit in disguise by the east,

and enter by shaded west,
undressing our complicit feet,
stifling the landing, as with the take-off.
Even innocent pets suffer forced silence,
taught, or bribed into compliance.
'Oh what a tangled web we weave,
When first we practice to deceive.'

In Anticipation

Today, before my anniversary,
The tired sun descends reluctantly.
My impatience, a candle burning,
Watching that indolent thing stalling.
Between this and my watch dial,
Two indifferent objects have me on trial.

I stand to regard the parting sun waltz
Against my newly pawpaw-painted walls,
The mango branch scraping the metal roof,
The silvered iron fence poles standing aloof,
Their scrawny silhouette on the ground eyeing
Agitated palm fronds doing their thing.

As for me, there's no other way to say
Such frolicking's not for me today;
Weightier things attend my investment,
And a crescendo of excitement
Is mounting, which I can scarcely contain,
And I pray this gusty wind bears no rain.

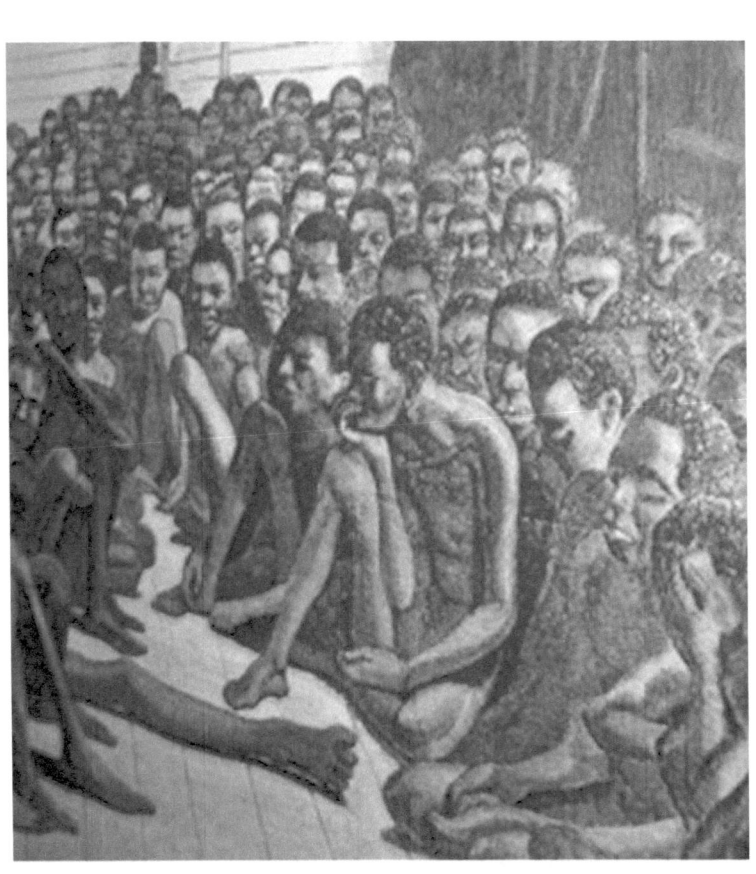

Metamorphosis

The shorn mind staggers toward alertness,
stunned by the spectral film of amnesia,
of all that was identity and race;
names lost, of kith and kin, of friends, of place,
impelled into the stifling holds of ships;
day and night pass by without a glimpse of face,
except for our own, as in sealed coffins,
where I and other ill-fated captives,
affixed by clanging chains to each other,
allotted merely breathing space, or less,
are huddled and degenerating in filth,
like crumpled, dirty linen at childbirth.

Locked away, oblivious of time and place,
forever seems real on the clock of minds.
The heave and ho of men persisting,
miraculously, when there is no strength
left to breathe, and the suffocating stench,
swelled by hellish body and spatial heat,
dispatch dead Jonahs to the swirling sea.

Destination: New Orleans, Alabama,
Jamaica, St. Kitts, scattered West Indies,
so many, I must read to remember.
Nothing familiar, nothing I have known,
only shards of a past I can't connect.
I touch my face to see if I'm real:
a streak of wetness down my cheek, I taste salt.
A man in my own domain, I've never cried,
now, a thing of straw to be tossed about,
I'm weeping, weeping uncontrollably;
I weep for my tribe, weep for Africa,

for jungles, for deserts, the savannahs.
Where is Tomba, and Nzenga, and Shaka?
What impotence the gods of my forebears!

I process the image—shackles on my feet.
Bought, sold, traded. Now transferred, I'm branded.
Overwhelmed by toil and trepidation,
puckish insomnia, as if abetting,
keeps tugging at me till Matuta stirs.

II

I awake one morning, metamorphic,
to a sinister transfiguration—
minus the glorified status of Christ;
for I'm battered and bruised, a broken shell,
glued together by ancestral longings,
mirror images haunting my daydreams,
my halo, a mosaic of broken bones,
my vision blurred by the impulse to run,
or to melt with the shadow and be healed.
Through sinuous trails framed by foot and hoof,
we trudge between the maze of cotton and cane,
climb spindly palms, pluck cocoa from rusty trunks...
And then, the murmur of a strange-sounding word:
"FREEDOM!"
But being unschooled and amnesiac,
I can't grasp its substance; so I listen,
and listen, and keep my eyelids ajar—
until, one day, I hear Massa grousing—
something to do with paying money to brutes.
And then, one day, he throws me three pennies,
instead of the whip or my meagre meal.

III

Now, years have thinned into decades, and I
regard the transformation that is me,
I measure the distance I have traveled,
the old order dismantled. I obey
new rules designed by popular mandate,
designate who to govern over me,
free to come and go without restriction.
Yet I think my freedom still elusive:
for while I know I have it in my grasp—
every statute states so in black and white—
I sometimes feel I breathe residual air
of centuries when we were all in chains.

Perhaps it's the old order that's returned,
dressed in neocolonial apparel,
fronted by old schoolmates we once trusted,
bounty hunters, as in the old homeland,
when our brothers gave us up for reward.

Speak to Me

Speak to me
spirit of elders
recount to me
in native idioms and metaphors
tales of erstwhile glory
lead me again
on the elongated neck of zebras
back to ancient rivers
where we flirted and floated
on compliant tree trunks
dancing with gamboling fish
we speared
out of an abundance
of gaiety

Speak to me
distressed spirits
of my forebears
tell me names
of ancients unrecorded
of battles
of conquests
of rituals
of journeys into manhood
of faiths older than Abraham's beard

Tell me
you sleep-walking spirits
tell me
that I may in turn
recount to my age
map out the footprints
in the borrowed language
of slave masters

in the tongue we fashioned
when the drum lost its speech

Speak to me
immortal spirits
imbue me
with the wisdom of centuries
of a time
when we strutted this Earth alone
impart the ways of Ma'at
anoint me a delegate
empowered to tear hearts open
to plant therein
the spirit we knew
the spirit
that has taken us the distance
the spirit
and wisdom
of Mandela
empower me
to transfuse into hearts
the blood of thoroughbreds
the revelation of tradition
the condition of reconciliation
the unification
of man and nation

Impasse

A case of fair weather
suddenly turning gray.
Remember our childhood chant
when, in scorching sun, it rained?
'Soley cho, lapli kwévé
Djab ka mayé dèyè kay'.
A fiendish gust of wind
blows the flies off my glass
but dust blocks my vision.
Jolted, my thoughts congeal.

I remember only saying
I won't bother to define—
I assumed we all knew
the word 'desecration';
I'd just pointed to Soufriere
to what was taking place there:
backhoes and bulldozers
dancing in cemeteries;
unearthed bones of ancients
petroglyphs and artifacts—
museum stock, or left untouched.
That's what the civilized do.
Not whoring for foreign bucks
risking accolades. That sucks!

This here poem's a preterm
for the storm raged more furious
and I, fearing the outdoors
in such ominous weather
surrendered to quibbling
to forestall caving in.

And though marked by incompletion
Yet I must make this insertion.
It's a dark side of us we show
Of a habit we seem to grow:
That what others are dying to save
We trade off like disabled slaves.

Vieux Fort Revisited

Ah, my old town,
how the times have changed!

The American is gone, decades now.
Gone, the reassuring sight of Uncle Sam uniforms,
semi-clad lads chasing after army jeeps,
no more the disquieting chants of 'Gimme a black penny, Joe!'

Indeed, how the times have changed!
No more the overflow at Four Winds,
Chè Bamboo, Kay Base-la.
Gone, too, the abundance of gaiety,
the ostentatious flash of Yankee dollars
for hired fare, or to light a cigarette,
ultimate metaphor for plenty
in the midst of poverty.
Gone, the 'rosy-cheeks-and-kankan' *djanmèts*
circling the soldier's glass like a tsetse fly,
the bounty-hunting avalanche of tradesmen,
—and others without trade, hunting all the same—
that swooped down from unheard corners.
Gone, the ready sale of overpriced goods,
and tradeoffs for good 'rejects' salvaged from camp.

The elders make me remember
The bittersweetness of the era:
a man shot to death by a soldier keeping guard,
compunctionless as one downs a blackbird,
because he would not keep out his dog;
the anxious moments at nightfall, at the balls,
when men feared losing their women;
the internecine bouts between trigger and switchblade,
byproducts not frequently recalled,
but not easily forgotten.

Yet, after the soldiers left, you sank into depression,
curtain half-drawn, you waited.
After all, they'd left much real estate behind.
But the American did not return.
So, unenthusiastically, you drifted back
to old occupations;
and those who did not fritter away their gains,
settled down to consolidate.

Recall the old airstrip that fissured with neglect,
that saw a hiatus of bovine infantry
tenanting a paradise of knee-high grass,
that made fat milking cows,
their bloated udders volunteering milk
you drew in bottles by 'the gate',
and the only landings were chutes of dung
that did not enrich the till.

The old order, centurywise,
bows to the paradigm of modernity.
Somnolent birds are startled
by the roar of other flying things,
descending through cracks in the weekend sky,
and what they drop, supposedly,
translates into greenbacks,
adjusting the bottom line.

Hewanorra, that was christened 'Beane Field',
welcomes another volley of customers,
vacationing Americans in Bermuda shorts,
and other tongues from other climes,
with nothing like war on their minds.

But as a land never short on surprises,
nearly all who deplane,
are shuttled over and across the Barre de L'isle,
to the designated Mecca up north,
unlike the forties Yankee who stayed,
to savour and alter your generosity,
of geography, of labour, of Adam's prick.

Today, plush new hotels stare, mostly vacant.
Today's *djanmèt* turned sex worker, turned zombie,
endures a leaner existence
than the competing, grudging taxi driver,
the feel of IN GOD WE TRUST being seasonal.

How many promises have you endured
since that frustrated man of God
took Christ's command at face value
shaking his dirty sandals in your face?
How many more curses will you suffer
'till you declare to yourself, 'The future's mine,
I'll take it from here'?

The Art of Poetry

It's easy to build monuments.
Midgets with time will pyramids.
Today's war needs no regiments.
Slaves have built empires of their own proceeds.

Poetry is a unique process.
It's not with what you have it's made,
But rather, from musing, or less,
When words fail or poetic elements fade.

Materials are cut and measured,
Each block or stroke must fit its plan;
With lyrics, it's not so structured.
Words comply, if steered by the mind, not hands.

Carnival

Each year, there comes a hot, hot season,
when stress and decency get undressed,
and sizzling women derrières get bared,
and rum-charged men wind on arse for free:
a carnival of flesh hooked on flesh,
ostensibly a cultural display,
a showcase of creative talent—
in reality, a corruption
of what the tradition first ordained.

Carne vale spelt goodbye to flesh.
Now bacchanalia dishes out flesh
squeezed into scanty imported tights,
and more flesh is gobbled than ever
while it lasts, into the next season.
A redefinition, I perceive,
a reversal in the scheme of things,
Lent, a distant event, abandoned.

In this season of rank debauchery,
there are others waxing lyrical,
setting the stage, prompting the foreplay,
stoking the fire in the heat of things,
and by stiff degrees, tipping the scale,
from issues taboo to the raunchy,
the downgrading more deliberate
as free speech gets more American.

What it boils down to is simply this:
another yielding of our psyche,
a pandering to the Empire's fancy.
Shamelessly, to plug budgetary holes,
to upwardly adjust statistics,
we realign custom and habit,

reassign dates, to alter substance.
Malleability, decidedly,
now determines the colour of sin.

These Islands You See

When God gave these sea-battered lands
To the green natives he found there,
Hardy men who lived by their hands,
Roots affixed to this hemisphere,
He willed them the entire chain,
The sea they hug, all it contains.

Before parting, in his wisdom,
God sermonized on splintering,
Knowing the future, what was to come,
Recalling Adam's backsliding.
But being Carib and Arawak,
Things changed just as God turned his back.

These green natives fought each other,
Captured wives, enslaving husbands,
And just as Cain to his brother,
They spattered their God-given lands,
With the blood of conquest and greed,
Raiding each other when in need.

Soon, God intervened once again,
Landing another breed of man,
Different, from far away as Spain,
France, Portugal, Holland, England,
Who duped and forced another breed,
To slave and satisfy their need.

To these he then bequeathed once more,
These same, further exploited lands—
A lot debased by whip and gore,
Shackled like beasts at feet and hands.
And when their freedom they regained,
Still then, they were in part detained.

This blue-green chain of lands you see,
Once appendaged to other realms,
Retain bloodstains of colony,
Europe sewn tight between their seams.
Obedience to the legacy,
Prohibits common policy.

In time each went their separate ways,
Breaking the chain of unity;
Confederate for a few short days,
Reverting to singularity.
The largest, being resourceful, went,
The puny left for selves to fend.

Alas, each Massa left his tongue,
A parting gift—the ultimate;
Their own, clay-smoothed, forgotten long
Ago on those doggone estates.
And being by language separate,
Their commonwealth disintegrates.

Cruiser

This crescent piece of real estate—
Only one free for miles around,

Its rocks, like steppingstones, of late,
Keep me rooted on solid ground;

Other stones, smoothed by the rolling,
Speak the dialect of growing up:

Shake off gathering moss by moving—
Death is occasioned when you stop.

Seashells vary, but all so bleached,
Are more than mere collectibles,

Encasing life before they were beached,
They've learned change is inevitable;

Like every trunk lying lifeless,
Cemeteried, as it were, in sand,

That flourished, fruited perhaps, impressed,
Being once a member of the band.

The sandpiper, sprightly cruiser,
Quick to spot trash from what it feeds,

Looks out for Skip, the beachcomber,
Hands deep in sand or dead seaweed.

The eye squints at unsightly lumps—
Our filthy deposits disgorged;

Sea and nature brutally stumped
By shit they refuse to dislodge.

Bent fishermen in wood canoes,
Sails and nets and such they're mending,

Their minds preoccupied, who knows,
With what tomorrow's weather'll bring.

Unnatural craters in the sand,
Truckloads smuggled by heedless ghosts;

My thoughts sink into the hole, and
Searching for words, this cruiser's lost.

Looking for Me in My Poetry

Sometimes, in my narrative—
often depending on what mood
I happen to be in at the time—
if you're perceptive enough
you can distinguish the writer
as protagonist or narrator.

Sometimes, in my narrative
I'm neither, but fretted within
hovering spiritedly over
strutting between lines and theme.
That may befuddle you somewhat
more so if you seek me where I'm not.

Sometimes, in my narrative
you'll find inquisitive pebbles
interposing between my lyrics
instigating dissonance.
They're hard to ignore, those bastards.
Just push them aside; they're such hazards.

Carpe Diem

I have learned, each day is different,
saddled as it is, with fragments
of reminiscences and long
forgotten snippets of sad songs;

or, a winged platform, that pauses
at every man's doorstep for his
turn to punch the mark on his forehead,
that says, he stood and was counted.

And as no two days are alike,
each match that you hold out to strike,
is set to ignite a new fire,
to light the way to what you'll acquire.

I've learned, as each day is different,
there's urgency in the moment.
And though there may be tomorrow,
the question is: How do we know?

Anse Ger Anger

A young country lad, so I'm told,
Not yet in CXC, not that old,
Decided to play God one day.
Upset, he took his life away.

All seemed okay at school that day,
He worked his math, joined the horseplay;
Later, on their way home from school,
Teased and guffawed, everything cool.

Back at home, no friends there to see
The darker side of reality—
Issues there to confront each day.
And being home, says you've got to stay,
Can't turn your back, just walk away.

Later, it's spilled in the media,
Of a dislike for his mother's
Manner of quelling some matter,
Favouring the love of his brother.

This unsettling act, entailed, they say,
Preferential love by Mom that day,
To an unwedded outsider
Over her son who loved her.

Silently, with pent-up anger,
The distraught lad cared no longer,
And knowing where the bottled poison laid,
Imbibed, and all vexations paid.

Castries From the Morne

Ideally, one can view Castries from the Morne,
standing near a monolithic relic
that sits idling in neutral,
because its tense is written
in stanzas of a dead empire.

Poised between clusters of bloodied flamboyant
and pregnant branches of *mango long*,
the eye captures the panorama
engirdling a basin of salt—
a harbour fatedly present
when history was shaking this isle
from obscurity and somnolence;
that witnessed unsettling exchanges
by rivaling expansionist invaders;
a nook where freighters sat out a storm,
until the Umptata was blown to smithereens;
yet it bears its badge with honour:
'*haud malefida carinis*',
a secure anchorage for ships.

To gaze down at this city this morning,
lying coolly beside the translucent sea,
void of its quota of mega cruisers,
it speaks in dialects of death,
of a thing portentously asleep.
Speckled by pockets of coal pit smoke
trailing over La Pansee from Babonneau,
the thurifer's swing over a black catafalque,
visits the memory, back to my acolyte days.

But on a clear day, when the mist has melted
and Phoebus' bright car is unblanketed,
stewing Vigie's cape, and Cap and Gros Islet,
the heart of town, Faux-a-Chaud, and all the way
past the exuberant blue-green hills of Monier,
there's hardly a comparable spot,
from which to take a memory shot.

The Ambivalent Tourist

This debutant English high-class
strapped like Siamese twins to his seat
peers through the elliptical glass
seeking the scenery through the mist.
The still, wooded topography
sends dark waves to his Bedford brain:
'What humans could conceivably
endure such claustrophobic terrain?'

At six thousand feet above ground
clouds step in to prevent your view;
you ask: paradise lost, or found?
That's what anxiety does to you.

For him, vision is limited,
only things familiar in his head:
storeyed steel and stone monoliths
caterpillars gliding on iron sticks
inner-city double-deckers
that get life from overhead wires
traffic thick like buffalo skin—
scenes that come naturally to him.

Suddenly, a new reality
creeps in, jerking him, abruptly:
perhaps he's being unreasonable?
Why had he endured such trouble
browsing piles of colour brochures
salivating on sights in pictures
dreaming erotic adventures
soaking alluring tales from friends
returning with their chocolate tans?

Adjusting his posture, slightly
he gulps his last swig of whisky
dons Rayban shades, feeling swanky
he shifts focus, new spirit turned on.
A voice blares from the intercom:
'Ladies and gentlemen
please fasten your seat belts.
We are about to land...'

And our man replies with gusto:
'Hi, Caribbean, here I come. Let's go!'

Rain Culture

Today was wet with God's generosity,
as He left the taps open, purposely,
as if to compensate for these past weeks,
when a roasting heat burned the skin like licks.

It's amazing, what a great leveller's rain;
bourgeois or *maléwé* obey each grain,
whether perforce, you bear it and get soaked
or not wishing to melt, you get cloaked.

An old habit Lucians treasure with rain,
a gastronomic thing we can't restrain:
a hot *bouillon's* best when forced indoors—
you'll down another's before sampling yours;

Lazy bums' excuse for sleeping longer,
they'll roll over to the sound of thunder.
The 'bossman' forgives staff who don't show up;
he too understands, when the covers drop.

Pouring rain's such a great aphrodisiac.
Just call any West Indian male and ask,
if he'll not prevaricate, and talk plain:
how many births he's had on account of rain?

They Laid Him in the Grave

As potent as the Nile's swelling,
a light shot across the canteen floor;
the noise it originated,
brought down its target, Orion.
And the darkness writhed in despair.

Unbelieving, I searched the dark,
custodians of the strangest of nights
preventing sleep's unwashed face.
Tormented, I prayed all night long,
for my daughter across the room.

The rain came down, as expected.
Naturally, I reminded Chelsea,
of the signals it always sends
at each significant moment.
And today was no exception.

This time I feared the outpouring,
perhaps it might keep mourners away.
A soggy ground at the graveside,
a pool in that desolate pit,
would disembalm the corpse, I thought.

The catafalque bearing your load,
and the Trident you once saluted,
stood rigidly at attention
as your book of life was opened;
they orated over the lines.

Would a soldier turn on himself,
with a decisive victory in sight?
I can't imagine a Caesar
dithering to cross the Rubicon,
spurred on by Senate and Pompey.

When the sound of hello's not heard,
it can be daunting to say goodbye.
Standing behind a half-closed door,
only ambient whispers seep through.
You slip by with the soughing wind.

I mourn the empty space endured
and conversations we might have had.
No motive, and cause without substance,
attends the illogic of men.
Thanks, to the mother who shaped you.

Bitter Bread

A man at table contemplates,
Salt tears drenching the bread he eats,
Recalling his world of former days;
The early tenants who held the keys,
Tended and helped to make it so,
Perhaps failing in one detail.
For he ponders a scenario,
Of much that's been struck and derailed:
Appointment of men of virtue
A rarity; the rest a slew
Posing as angels, donning wings,
Power-crazed despots clinging to things;
Falsity, shameless, sits enthroned
Next to conscience, dead, and vice, now cloned.

In this, Vespucci land's a principal,
Both fire and rain, Satan and archangel,
Smart hedonistic mind-bender,
High priest of immoral agenda,
Pacifier and arms dealer,
Opportunist power broker.
Foisting Superman's way its métier,
The big apple that spawns decay.

Thus, a man may eat bread buttered by Yanks,
But knowing, perhaps should say 'No thanks'.

WAKONTE
COMIC BOOKS

soucoyan

Painting by Alwyn St. Omer

Death of a Soukouyan

Man Épiphane Déwivyè die,
An' you could see it in de sky.

Same hour de news begin to spread,
How dat evil *gajé* was dead,

Clouds turn from gray to sooty black;
Dogs in de 'hood begin to bark;

Birds of all shape an' description,
Shoot like arrow out de region—

Like when firework burst at New Year's,
An' dogs yelp an' scamper in fear.

Soon, neighbours begin to gather,
But speaking only in a whisper,

An' frighten to enter de house,
Knowing de trade of de ole louse.

But in curious irony,
De entire community

Have dis one common agenda:
One las' look at de *soukouyan*.

An' when, later, as is custom,
Mourners would chant an' down white rum,

Dance *bèllè kont*, an' tell ole jokes,
Is *silans*—like lockjaw grip de folks.

Is first wake I ever witness,
Where people make no *mové mès;*

Where rum, biscuit an' coffee pass,
An' behaviour like is high-class.

But it ain't no class ting, believe me,
It ain't no 'Hoitee an' Toitee'.

Is 'fraid dey 'fraid *Ma Déwivyè,*
Dat ole *gajé* from *Gwan Wivyè.*

An' think I forget de coffin,
De las' bed dey lay de witch in?

Dey say, inside de cemetery,
She demonstrate some devilry:

De coffin spin twice near de hole,
Just as de church bell start to toll.

An' as dey sling her down de hole,
Dere was a noise like thunder roll.

People stop singing *Libera,*
An' start making de *sin-a-kwa.*

De priest sprinkle holy water,
An' say some abracadabra.

Den dey plaster de bitch with dirt,
Axing her broomstick reign on earth.

Folks say de priest was too damn *boleface,*
To give she de rites in de first place.

Without Grace
(For Sister Theresa and Leota)

She came
and like the wind
is gone
leaving traces
only cherished memories
footprints in the hearts
and minds of those who knew her
of those who loved her.

We had no time
no time at all
to appreciate in life
the good she was
the good she brought
the joy to share
the treasure buried
in her virgin breast.

She embraced the world
loved it
served it.
Her celibacy
her key asset
sanctioned trophy
is gone too
forever lost.

That fateful day
sometime in May
a loose boulder
losing its grip, and swift
like a vulture, wild
or a chicken hawk, pouncing

crashed upon the innocent
unwary teacher
with an assassin's poundage.

The world, then
recoiling
upsetting
saw her go
white and bloodied.

And we, standing
kneeling
try to reach her shore.
But the tide keeps pulling...
                    pulling...
                            pulling...

Country Night

Boukan flaming
Cricket crackling
Klac-klac clacking
Bètafé illuminating
Flanbo blazing
Oil lamp flickering
Crapaud leaping
Darkness thickening
Stars scintillating
Bedding spreading
Tim-Tim: storytelling
Jans gajé frightening
Zombi flying
Konpè Lapen scheming
Konpè Tig conniving
Baby slumbering
Rain intermitting
Roof percussioning
Music enchanting
Now the world's transmuting.

What? Someone snoring?

Silent Killers

In the ambience of dusk,
woodworms take a pause from work
to digest invaded stock,

huddled tight like dentures
within the hollowed fissures,
they burp and choke on whispers.

The green ones, deficient,
capacity still latent,
sniff the sweet resin, rest content.

A meal indeed they make,
vermin we consider weak,
of fortresses we erect.

History's tales resound:
empires are built or brought down,
not by kings, but their minions.

Ditto

Sometimes, in a moment of utter calm,
I swear I can hear the blue hills wail,
uttering a sound, like when the spindly palm
is caught in a storm and tries to un-nail
its tortured branches from the wind's torment;
as when a blue marlin knows that moment
when its fate is not negotiable. That's when
I rise, and dress to welcome a new day,
and greeted, instead, by news of death, again:
someone fed a stew of lead, on the Chaussee,
or the glint of metal returns, bloodied,
from a raid, or to avenge something stupid.

Will anger, or *tabanka*, trail the same weird path,
condemned, like slaves, to serve the ego
that never shows up when reason confronts Earth,
and robed Justice inks the entry: Ditto?
My soul recoils at the weakness of past slaves—
the masturbatory response on the airwaves.

Clarke Street, Vieux Fort

It's an eel stretched its full length:
you enter its open mouth
into the womb of this town,
down to its fish-tagged tail
to where the old jetty lay.

Its customized eyes that see
all traffic that come and go,
suggests a second rebirth,
altogether dismissive
of a forgotten traffic
—north to the runway, and south
of the dissecting highway—
when sugar cane was king, and
whose rusting iron rails you'll find
back of the square and beyond.

Save for Beane Field's recent fuss,
all life seems compressed to fit
into this linear space,
like a string of black pudding:
petrol station, bank and school;
struggling boutiques, mini marts;
spot where *Book Nook* used to be—
pioneer bookstore for years;
a non-compliant array
of fish and produce vendors;
hucksters of second-hand goods;
watering holes, smoking stands of roast,
the creature's belly swelling,
with bodies from Grace, Belle Vue,
bargain seekers from Soufriere,
when spending soars at week's end.

Thoroughfare dissector too,
of this fatigued-looking place:
Bacadere and The Dengue,
West End, moribund marketplace,
legendary hill with the cross,
where the priest shook his sandals
and a town is forever cursed;
the misnomer 'Commercial Street',
Belvedere, home of 'Mothers',
first schools, *fijé* and *bèbel*;
'Bridge Street' relieved of meaning,
that sleeps with a cemetery,
all lying lazily to the west;
and to the expanding east,
Louisville and *Bò Lizin*,
The Mangue that stifled with rage,
till *Shine Drive* opened a vent
to see through Beane Field and Bruceville,
a saunter 'cross New Dock Road;
the whole of that clustered lot
to where a cadaverous *Clouds Nest*,
perched, ghost-like atop a hill,
peers down to the dying *Cocodan*.
Halved like A.D. and B.C.,
all's east, or west of Clarke Street.

Despite its altering visage,
some old staples linger on,
granitic with defiance:
the accommodating steps
at Boriel's palatial set,
that's warmed many a backside;
Green's grocery, most legendary,
essential to the history;
a sprawling fishery landing,
struggling to play by the rules,

sneers at hagglers roadside by *Bruce*;
and the most incongruous sidewalks,
are found one side of Clarke Street.

Other things historical,
have left footprints on this scape:
ask Ma Romain's verandah
that equates Castries Market Steps,
what decibels it survived
the firebranding from *Odlum*,
Josie, Chandelle, Etoile stalwarts;
strut southward, was Ma Gilbot's
or Leo Victor's rum shop,
or a short distance even,
stood a rough-hewn concrete slab
in front Mederick's select pub,
that hosted *Flambeau* rivals—
Compie, flamboyant *Fred Astaire*,
diminutive *Dada Riviere*...
Memories transparent as ice,
recall the most iconic
mal manman, with his fruit tray
just lower Sibot's bakery,
next to San Nicolas' Bar.

Now, on a personal note,
I'm compelled to do justice
to a memory I cling to,
of Jones' upper floor outfit,
Golden Arms Restaurant and Bar,
where buddy Norbie and I,
after 11.30 Mass,
stomped the stairs for best rum punch,
or a personalized roti.

And of course, before Clarke Street,
there was *Malgretout-Micoud Road!*—
struck me as a dumb-ass name.
I can still picture the sign
above the gray wooden house,
across Boriel's and the cross,
where two light-skin virgins lived...

I can see the small chalkboard,
nailed to a lamppost, like Christ,
where *Izik* marked for *Fwèto*
in fine calligraphic style,
Hollywood's latest release
at the *Flying Hawk's Cinema:*
Liz Taylor, Richard Burton,
starring in *Cleopatra;*
Yul Brynner and Steve Mc Quinn—
The Magnificent Seven;
Roy Rogers and...can't remember—
Don't Fence Me In, that I loved.
And youths diversely focused,
huddled like flies to salivate,
thinking of a seat in *Pit*,
or better, *Circle*, with nuts,
next to a girl, if lucky.

It was here, decades ago,
in the enlightening sixties,
or the *kann-kannese* fifties,
Tota's horse-driven buggy
began the rounds for garbage;
here, too, *Bedfords, Thames, Austins*,
started the arduous trek north—
smart in colour and names, as
the designer wooden frames

that stunned their British makers:
Trojan, Sputnik, Morning Fly,
adeptly conducted by
Fergis, the Tobierre's, *Fwèto*;
yet others won't be outdone,
like young stargazing *Nornos'*
top-notch *Stella Polaris*,
while Mister Mike, with Success,
conveniently unhurried:
last to depart, last train in.
But that's stuff for the archives…

Believe it when I tell you,
If Clarke Street were a shoe,
Not many feet would fit in,
For things it's been and seen.

Dusk in the Cemetery

There lies the old elegiac cemetery
at the edge of this town courted by two seas
at the edge of an acquiescent river
where clawed crustaceans edge in for a living
where once, only those who'd smoothed the kneelers
were interred with full rites. And the French priest
bids farewell: "Requiescat in pace".
There, after Phoebus' car has waved au revoir
and green-flashed into its diurnal dive—
only to resurrect next morning
on the other side of this sleepy town
and remain hung overhead, like Ma Cass'
rainbow coalition of flagging laundry—
tenants, waiting for Christ, stretch their stiff limbs
change position one more time
and resume their asphyxiated sleep of death.
A lapsed town, a dead cemetery, side by side
symbiotically, reflecting a state.

Mount Gimie

3,145 feet,
clouds sail past like U.S. drones,
almost reachable,
all of Lucia below and beyond,
every God-blest peak,
not a shrub out of vision,
the distant sheet of blue
illusively frozen.

But what's that burning scent I smell?
Amazona Versicolor,
king of all he surveys,
circles once, twice,
signals an old *soupsyon*—
I'm moved to think...

Oh, perish the thought, says *Jacquot*.
It's nothing burning.
It's the sweet scent of Mary Jane.
'*Polis mouté Mòn Gimie*
Vini fè kouyonté...'

At a height like this,
a high like that
must be the ultimate high.
How much closer to a deity
who made it all and deemed it good,
can one ever wish to get?

At a height like this,
with smoke and cloud in your eyes,
vision blurred, yet couldn't be clearer,
lyrical scripture on your lips,
you can virtually engage God.

The essential smoke that rises,
validates the *Idren*'s belief,
it's ritual, it's biblical.

3,145 feet,
above man and beast,
dwelling place of God and the blest—
not the locus of *kouyonté*,
nor man-appointed *movèzté*.

An bel ti plas kon Mòn Gimie...

Moule-a-Chique

So this is it—
that other leg of deep south,
standing tall and proud, that predates
the valley nestled in your shadow,
that demands a Boy Scout's hike,
for the steep descent that separates you.

From this awesome perch,
I see Aktukan remarking
the waves' untiring chatter below,
the East Trades stiffening his visage,
as he confidently surveys
that vast expanse he claims,
two oceans lying at his feet—
from breezy Beane Field to the hushed Black Bay,
the dense, woody mangrove hideout,
egret and crab sanctuary
that we christen Mankotè.
Barely batting an eyelid,
the Carib chieftain peers north to
Au Picon, Pierrot, Morne Cayenne,
sweeping the craggy outline of Pointe des Kayes,
then westward, to Laborie, Choiseul,
a knot of misty blue hills,
habitation of kindred tribes.

Now, it's my turn to revel
in the euphoria of ownership,
the joy of knowing that I, too,
can claim all that you proclaim,
all that you stoutly dominate,
home to this cyclopean icon
twice beacon, for land and sea,
history's burden attenuated.

What monarch, being sane,
would dither with an army
to capture or defend a prize
so unparalleled?
The remnants abound,
loud in yesterday's assessment
of all that you stand for,
as others, through naked eye
or fancy gadgets capturing,
genuflect, like Moses, to hail:
this is holy ground.

So why should I surrender
either a jot of your clay,
or the wonder that softens
this unyielding piece of clay?

No Child's Play

Sometimes, one's world is visited
by a tsunamic twist of fate;
no truce, no allied intervention
can deflate a swollen psyche
to stem the slide to the abyss.

I understand, perfectly,
that Gethsemanic feeling,
when the crushing weight of cares
appeals to a chasm, to descend,
to delete the image of Christ,
to usurp his destined place,
to utter, *sans parole*,
it is finished,
I return what you gave,
your indigestible pottage
laced with Jacob's self-serving shit.

I peer through the sheet of glass,
through fake barrier stifling truth,
to confront hate, rejection,
failure insecurely nestled,
destined for absolution failure.
No godfather there to cuddle;
bosom friends denied access,
the kindred will find out, in time.

Frequently, it's the vicious trap
of quotidian or sudden stress,
that irrepressible drug,
the sin of self-elimination,
that leaves soul mates in a whirl,
rumour mongers to speculate.

More Than Dogs

(*The more I learn about people,
the more I like my dog*—Mark Twain)

Humans are innately
Creatures of emotion;
They show an uncanny
Likeness to dogs, in exception.

A dog may faithfully
Guard a man and his turf;
Yet the same will viciously
Rip master like a piece of cloth.

Men will feign sympathy,
Nay, shed crocodile tears,
While your obituary
Is dancing beneath the layers.

Don't leave your coat hanging
Where Homo sapiens prowl;
And when you're out walking,
By no means do so cheek by jowl.

Still, exude tolerance,
Don't attend unkindness
With silly remonstrance;
Let asses slurp their own *konmès*.

What Is I.S.?

Who or what IS that behemoth,
Janus, in-your-face leviathan,
stomping across Saddam's remains,
obliterating Assad's footprints,
that holds the living manacled,
a world, coalitioned, impotent?

Who or what IS that beast, soulless,
armed with bullet and a faith,
beheading nations for a state,
relieving captives of their head,
extending its bionic arms,
extinguishing village lights,
defoliating trees at a shot,
emptying communes of child content,
Attila the Hun all over?

Who or what IS it, defiant,
heedless of reason but its own,
mocking the darling metaphor
—the image of bird in a cage—
to roast, encaged, while he yet breathed,
a flying meal on a mission,
hapless, losing his wings in flight,
the world horrified, spectating?

Who or what IS that pariah,
bloody and bloodying, wallowing
in a theatre of savagery?
Who or what IS that mean, er, thing,
that values not life nor fears death,
that will be God and Lucifer?

Oh history, thou art brute,
Flipping the pages of memory,
Dancing to drum and flute,
Nero's Rome ablaze with fury.
Arise, sleeping giant!
Cancel the pause for peace, Japan!
Delete this ugly narrative,
Make this poem a make-believe.

(February 4, 2015, a pilot was caged and burned alive by ISIS)

Old and New

Suddenly, I feeling old
beside dem modern youth
flagging dey high tech ting in me face;
dey ears plugged off from de rest of de world
wires round dey neck like a medic
dey have no use for shoelace
dey feet stuffed in fancy Gear—
a texting, WhatsApp-ing generation, I fear.

Me, I from anudda age, poupa Jesus!
I born when a house was ajoupa
tile and galvanize didn't invent yet;
tèsson was stove
pressure cooker was *kanawi*
only bouj had fridge in Sènt Lisi
a *kawaf* was perfect
if cold water was your fancy
kalbas fetched river water
to break one was disaster.

When dey was one pharmacy
most everyone, literally
knew de herbs had potency:
djapanna, chapantyé
chadon benni, koupyé;
and a rub down would leave you
smelling of hospital or *sendou*
but it work.

Hand-me-down was 'ration'
but still common;
eating fresh was tradition:
ti ditèn, agouman, ti lonyon
spiced up a pumpkin-beef *bouyon*

85

folks said dat was good for de young;
TV and technology
did not separate family
life was marked by paucity
but folks were content and happy.

Nutten remain de same
each new age bring its own shame.

I laugh every year
when October come
seeing dem same youth
hustling dey granma
to view and sample
de same old things
dem jeer at and criticize
making me feel old and stupid.

Photo by Vincent Berquez

Reply to Vincent Berquez's *Vivienne*

Mad girl from other ward
Laughs and bangs on the wall.
Mad girl from other ward
Screams and then I hear her fall.
Mad girl from other ward
Ups and asks me for a buck:
I pause.
Mad girl from other ward
Stomps and says she wants a smoke:
I help her cause.

(*I met Berquez online in April, 2015*)

Imagined

where have you been all my life?
I've been countless days
and countless nights
alone unthinking evil thoughts
deleting mischievous imaginings of you
with another woman

where have you spent your decades
of dry and lonesome years
without the warmth of a body like mine
angling this way then that
fidgeting with tear drenched pillows
and in the dew-dropped morning
can't find your fingers
to open the bathroom door?

where have you been
all these unmarked
pages of almanacs
when August storms raged
shooting volley upon volley
of bullets of rain
on my stuttering galvanize plates
tearing off like leaves
from the succumbing glory cedar
enriching my neighbour's stock
down the block
and I
drenched like Tuesday laundry
rolled in plastic
mummified in the closet
trying to remain standing
picturing with misdirected concern
the pliant palm trees outdoors

humiliated like bullied schoolboys?
For decades unending
I've been alone
living with visions of you
in every fleeting shadow
in every pair of fluttering eyes
that stared back.

I've had more storms
than Italy can count elections
felt more pain than Panadol remembers
seen more droughts than the Sahara.
I've forgotten the taste of water
the smell of dewdrops
the sound of evening descending.

Without you by my side
I've groped without touching
learned to find meaning
meaning in dying
dying to be free
free from the torment of you
you melting in the embrace
of another woman
of my imagining.

Lesson Learned

I once had dreams
of platforming my dreams
in an open forum
like an urban street
marked No Entry
or in camera somewhere
at the break of dawn brainstorming
admitting members only.

I once confrered
with the brightest and best
inputting and scripting
all ideas contending
open and free
imbibing the same vibe
unfazed by perceived diatribe
set to upset plutocracy.

I once had dreams
of a bright day dawning
of a disemboweled past
of new beginnings
a proud citizenry
six is six, nine is nine
no one gets stuck on the lifeline
equal opportunity.

I once had dreams
I once had visions
baked in an oven of fantasy.
I woke up dazed, bruised and empty
no victory, no spoils, no trophy.
Now I will never sleep again
fearing to dream and dream in vain.
I will stay up and watch the History
    Channel.

A Black Bay Sunset

Through a door left ajar
I was utterly floored
by this momentary beauty—
the blue-green hills of Black Bay
changing face
donning gray all at once
overwhelmed by the munificence
of a declining mid-April sun
offloading its brilliance
enveloping the landscape
as would a billowing cloud
from a sylvan charcoal pit.

The intensity of the glow!
The momentary dimming
then re-incandescence—
an absolute frontispiece
for my next book, I thought—
as intervening clouds
sought to dull the image
without succeeding
the mass transmuting to a haze
visible only with a squint.

I watched speechless
for what seemed a prolonged display
choreographed
for my singular enjoyment
imbibing the magic and mystery
of nature's artistry
feeling blessed.

I watched the same episode
replayed for days, undeterred
by the roguish grief of rain
or the depressing sighing of clouds.
Is there another audience somewhere
I wondered at last
spectating
theatre directed by angels?

Downcast

I swooped down like a famished *kayal*
riding Jesus' handpicked ass—
the one he rode into Jerusalem
treading on palms and women's *mouchoirs*
amid a cacophony of hosannahs
he could scarcely hear the Holy Ghost—
and circled your 'hood like a ritual
your head spinning like a top
in anticipation
eager to drink from my gourd
brimming with 'Promise Wine'.

I came—like Beewee's test landing
that enlivened old Beane Field's tarmac
shaking a town from somnolence—
strapped on my athletic back
Santa's backpack I borrowed
chock full of hopes and promises
certain plans and strategies
and you, burdened with despair
disinterred dreams of two lifetimes
impatient like kids at Christmas Eve
eyes glued like *pwalud* to my sack...

After pursuing your comfort faithfully
neglectful of self and progeny
after I've been sapped
like Ezekiel's dry bones
you have the nerve to reproach me
hurling shrapnel of ingratitude
aiming to crucify me
your once christened 'Messiah'
only because I did not deliver
on your one small miracle—

squeezing blood out of stone.
But I return, my conscience clear
knowing my one motive was your good.
Your searing ingratitude I absolve.

It's Not the Same

I sit atop an old oil drum,
somewhat precariously,
observing youngsters at play;
what they are playing at
is engaging much brain and brawn,
thumping and pushing buttons, keys,
competing with programmed intelligence,
dueling to control a cyborg
for points:
GO...OVER...UNDER...STOP!
faces distort with anger
when they suffer defeat.

I take the long look back to
when we didn't live in two worlds.
I see the same kids—
playing.

Flamboyant

A red flamboyant in blossom
is an arrogant creature.
It holds its basin of blood
in mid air for a show,
until it sheds it all,
like a crucified Christ,
drop by redeeming drop,
its petals a red pool,
smearing the ground at its feet.

The Addict

They scarcely avert the limelight now:
disciples of the trade
whose day begins with a ritual of grass
who can't function without it.

This one I espy at early dawn
in absolute ecstasy
long before his first puff
and each time he takes it in
sometimes impatiently a double drag
is a manifestation of contentment
mirror imaging the fed multitude
or an imitation of the ordained
presiding over the act
of transubstantiation
sanctifying bread and wine
offered again to the Father.

His gesture is a total commitment
his partaking a religious conviction;
completely oblivious of detractors
he drinks the chalice to the dregs
ending up looking levitated
starkly reminiscent of an ascetic monk.

Later
distracted by the necessity of work
he speeds out of his domicile
and with the dose of speed in him
he seems charged to take on the world.

Fanm Kankannez

Each time I pass,
her house next to mine,
the election road next to our house,
her whole body itches,
tout ko-i ka gwaté-i,
a paroxysm of it.

She craves unsolicited admission,
so she invents some distraction:
she quickly embraces her broom,
inviting it to a faked waltz,
where no speck of dust
even bothers to rise,
for indeed none exists there,
where she forces the broom to dance.

I heard of this gimmick,
years ago, from my mother,
or encountered a partisan of it,
somewhere in D.W.,
a custom nosey women adopt,
a cheap ploy to feign busyness,
when words take a back seat,
or she casts herself
in a play she herself has plotted.

The broom dances,
but does not participate,
for that's not in its nature
—though trash is its business—
not to sweep over a clean surface,
not to seek to raise dust
where no dust even cares to gather.

Subtly, she's upset with the broom;
she's upset there's no dust
to enliven her brainless little cause.
She's upset with me
for ignoring her existence.

Amazingly there's victory in silence.
Sometimes a battle is won
by not taking up arms.

Meditation

The Akkadian sauntered across the lawn
sheltered by the shade of proud acacia,
famed rendezvous of lovers and soldiers,
where stone benches are armed with such secrets
that might break a marriage or lose a war.

In solitude and pensive like Hamlet,
freshly reassigned on terra firma,
after months of brutal battles at sea
side by side with brave comrades of the trade,
he mused on how the Fates had favoured him.

Seven months he had endured both weather
and the despised enemies of his land,
yet he loved utterly his vocation,
a life he'd chosen since he was a boy,
and had accosted death many a day.

Countless men he'd seen cemeteried at sea;
battleships engulfed by furious waters,
as if accompliced with the enemy,
and though numbers depleted either way,
his memory jogged by scenes of heroism.

There were times, in the peak of engagement,
he pondered on the sanity of it,
the worth of settling conflicts in this way;
his thoughts shot back to those he'd left behind:
would there be the chance to see them again?

Quickly, he brushed aside such emotions,
mere distractions foreign to his métier;
if the fatherland must be defended,
or prestige or self-respect is challenged,
who but its sons to heed the bugle call?

His battle scars he carried like a badge,
he walked the streets with conspicuous pride,
respect greeted him wherever he went.
At last, piqued by the largesse of Nature,
he prayed inwardly for lives sacrificed.

Unstoppable

I'm a creature sanctioned to blow
unfettered wherever I go.

I'm the invisible hand, you know
I can move fast, I can move slow
I leave no trace, no shadow
crisscrossing hill and meadow.

I can soothe a burning day so
but I can put on quite a show
blow your mind, unhinge a window
shatter roof, uproot palm and mango
make oceans rage, waves billow
incite the wild to dance a tango.

I am smooth like a child's pillow
twice softer than marshmallow
I'm no mollycoddle, you know
unbridled, free to come and go.

I'm your feared nemesis, and oh
I love it when you whimper so
when you creep for cover below
your customized roof I'll soon blow.

A lamb today, wolf tomorrow
enigmatic, like MP so-and-so
I will help make a fire glow
or charge it to char a town. Yahoo!

And speaking of town, apropos
I can alter the status quo
make the wealthy poor while on the go
unify all to a calm plateau.

I am ever-present wind.
Be sorry that you have sinned.

Another View of Storms

A thing of mystery it is
of twigs forcibly waltzing with pain
while generational palms, aiming heavenward
thirty feet of spindly trunk
arrogantly unbendable
crack the way wickets tumble at Lords
surrendering to invisible blades.

Avian neighbours, hapless
that were nesting in pliant branches
anticipating the torment
flee to safety in exile
while the storm performs its orchestral show:
full-blown blasts echo like deranged choristers
peals of thunder chipping in with the drumming
lightning bolts with full effect to show the stage
loose or loosening galvanize overhead
providing percussion and rhythm
marking a landscape for intensive care.

Moments after the announced abatement
the manifestly half spent retiree
alive thus far by grace and mercy
emerges from his den of penitence
emulating Noah, assessing the damage
occurring smack in this hard guava season
calculating the certain dent on his purse.

Awestruck by the storm's damning rage
that has ravaged much around me
I am convinced how much He cares
seeing an entire roof
not too long mounted
lifted like a paper kite

while mine I feared would comply with a kiss
threaded the eye as it passed.
I marvel at obnoxious pretenders
making light of the bashing
blasphemously absolving the drama
as though they could do with another storm.

Savouring Sunday Silence

Uncaring of the day or the hour
Miscreants stripped of the plate of conscience
Drive noisy things over the agéd's dower—
Contrasting generations, in essence.

Sundays were reserved, in seasons gone by
For thanksgiving, the wearing of new suits
For doing together things and getting high
On beef and pumpkin soup and English fruits.

Now saving the silence has come to mean
Idleness—the work of geriatrics.
Youth can't savour servings of calm and clean
They bask instead in noisome, risky tricks.

Prophecy

Take these words
Read these words
Chew these words
Fold these words
Wrap these words
Gift these words

Open these words
Dissect these words
Debate these words
Fashion these words
Project these words
Respect these words

Take these words
Store these words
Lock these words
Frame these words
Hang these words
Watch these words
      unfold

The Earth is No Longer Young

The earth is no longer young.
Two billion years, three billion
by whatever calculation
is a statement about old age.

From Pleistocene to Paleocene
Jurassic to pre-Cambrian
settling into Homo sapiens
the evolution of brain
the orderly mix of white and gray
to the mysterious thread work we see
Man and mind have been around.
The wear and tear must spell declension
some might even say apoplectic
for thinking seems all but annulled.

How else to explain rationally
the condition of a fucked-up world
outrageously and permanently
screwed to the shadow of its decaying self
staring at real and imminent
threat of self-extinction?

Again, one asks, what callous mind
but a mind degenerated, decaying
could manufacture and impose
a poison christened 'Global Warming'
its antidote so uncertain
that demands unanimity
to even approve the label?

The earth is no longer young
our space now seems inadequate.
Yet as a species vastly endowed
to command life, to chart destinies
he's certainly dropped the ball.
Soon we may have to ingratiate the gods.

As time is the ultimate healer
We'll find the balance—sooner or later.

Finished

I am finished, absolutely finished.
Finished with all this imbecility
all this kiss-arse genuflecting for attention
this obsolescent kiss-and-make-peace pantomime
this charade of engineered mamaguism
this tyranny of servant over master
this defaulting on dismantled promises
void of sincerity in the first place
this load of *copain-copine* incestuousness
on the altar of favouritism;

I am through, absolutely finished.
Done with your copulatory work regime
your duplicate-pay-packet nepotism
your dim transparency of '*anba tab-ism*'
your highfalutin *découché* speechifying
—spectator bullshit-ism in fancy attire—
your inveigling, copious Houdinic crap in the House
when so many homes barely pass the test for houses
when others forcibly endure your spellbinding feat
and you repair to your comfort of air con and flat screen;

I'm finished, absolutely finished.
Finished being tricked to dance your tango
when La Woz and Magwit struggle to *bwiyé*
starved of oil to keep their wick burning
Cindarella-ed to that barren wench, Jazz
that guzzles wondrously more than it brews;
no more the one-sided crap of belt tightening
shamed by your shameless rotundity
because you don't have to strike for your pay
all dizzying stuff I wipe my dirty feet on;

I am done, absolutely finished.
Over with loud-mouthed hypocrisy
finished with wasting my tears over others' dead
or lending ear to bigots waving the Holy Book
or congregating with nitwits and Pharisees;
I am done drinking wine from broken vessels
in the sheer pretense of honouring a vow;
I spit on all sycophantic partisans
who milk the system for selfish advantage
and flaunt their wares as if of clean making;

I am finished, 'finito!' I repeat.
I wash my hands of party flags and symbols
finished with blood-stained fingers for cronies;
I spew my vomit on jump-on-bandwagonners
let me wait for the bus on the potholed highway;
I'm done too with gossipers and crooks for neighbours
I'll find my brother on the road to Jericho;
I'm through stifling my hate for Alabama
reinstated by overtly racist MIB
defiantly shooting down 'Black Lives Matter';

I am finished, decidedly over
with placatory niceties and vain talk
your torrents of piss-in-the-eye for rain
shooting your load on the teats of the arts
masturbating publicly without memory;
I'm done feeling angry like Derek
finished with expectations of finer things
things civilized people do for the arts
because you don't have a place for such in your heart.
Look now the bard has passed on, his prayer unanswered.

I am finished, undoubtedly finished.
Done with the filth from plebeian talk machines
garbage born out of malevolence and ignorance;

through with miserable, idling *makoumès*
calabash-headed imbeciles needful of a life
squandering valuable time playing *maco*.
Through with the typos lifting stones, looking for trash
while I watch through the trained eye of a seer
hear, without listening, with the locked ears of Beethoven
wiping their purulence staining Dunstan's moustache;

I reject with absolute finality
the minimization of Black by Black;
what do I care, if they do a Cain on their own?
Being heartless when they slaughter with dirty tricks
let Lucifer salivate on the vengeance to come.
I am pissed and done with dated rules
of behavior that make a mockery of courtesy:
greeting everyone you pass on the way
should not include the devil you know;
down with meaningless gestures the heart can't stomach;

I am finished, unrepentantly finished.
I am finished, I too am done with caring
whether you like me or hate my poetry
I will not compromise art for patronage
the lean sheep survives though summer grass be brown.
What I believe is no more of the innate
my faith now hinges on the a posteriori;
down with the fallacy of infallibility
see, Revisionism's blade is still bloody;
I cling to poetry, alone faithful in all seasons.

Ode to a Panman

The rubber-shod sticks
pound the quartered oil drum;
the arpeggios he articulates
translate a thematic narrative
that percolates the salt-tanged breeze
fanning the tailored fringes of the Plaza,
his alfresco theatre
in which he plays,
actor, director, ticket collector,
sometimes his own audience.

Forever the quintessential soloist,
he alone sets the score---
theme, tone, pace:
allegro or allegretto;
forte or fortissimo;
piano or pianissimo;
calypso, reggae,
Mozart, Beethoven,
mamay la-kaye;
whether in pampered monologue
narcissistically,
or couched in phrases to move a crowd,
his rendition strictly obedient to his baton,
indifferent to the East wind
seductively prying under the leafy skirts
of Beane Field's manicured sea-grapes.

Alas, he is silent now;
steely silent,
like the tenor pan he left in memoriam.

I see Shine airlifted by angels,
some gather like ants to form a ring;

I behold the master, Winston Spree Simon,
enfolding Mano in a tight embrace:
'Dah is yuh, Boggz!'
the other Master, in cheerful acknowledgement
advances to welcome a musical son
in whom he is well pleased.

As he lived and was sustained by music;
as music is the preferred food of the Muse,
let's play one for Mano.

Forced Labour

I'd vowed it would be my last poem.
The labouring gets ever tighter
mirror of the old wood-framed bus
that laboured up the Barre de L'isle
my lyrics are the paying passengers
breathing the filthy sweat of beasts
headed for the Castries slaughter house;
they resist being taken captive
and I do not wish to force them
to a life of uncertainty.
But I comply with the bidding
of the Muse, who's stronger than I.
What I do now is not of me
any more than the protagonist
can claim authorship of the book
or Lazarus be Christ, for his two lives.
This last initiative, I confess
conceived of boredom and fatigue—
the Devil has no hand in this—
simply had to be rendered free.

Meditation and the Cross

I stand alone, in the heart of a silent field,
A wooden cross signaling the last appointment;
All's dead or dying 'round me, save the periwinkle,
The choir singing Libera for him being interred.
The dug hole yawning, impatient, waits to swallow
The latest scoop of Adam's curse to all mortals,
Fed it by servitors of death, or fake mourners
That can't wait for the slinging and the rites' "Amen!"
To feast on bounteous servings of rum and hors d'oeuvres,
The incentive that enticed them in the first place.
Then after foul-mouthing the dead and family,
They head back to reinstate their status quo ante,
Unmindful of the departed plastered in the mud.

I cross myself, not to signal an act of faith,
But to ensure I do not abandon my post.
I hang around, pondering the capped candle burning:
With what stoic ease mortals adjust to dying!

The Mullah to his Disciple

Always expect the unexpected,
the Mullah said to his disciple;
nothing but the cold of death is certain.
It's not given to man to predict
that which he has no control over,
even when he thinks he knows the source.

Life is brewed out of vast elements,
ingredients poured into the mixing bowl,
stirred by the power of Mother Nature,
stored and simmered to a perfect blend;
and when at last, taken off the mold,
it goes out on a course unprogrammed.

The things and events we encounter,
are really chips from the main event,
making their own way, or tossed about
as products of accident or choice.
Though given life, they are let free to
control or be ruled by the winds of fate.

All things animate grow and come to rest,
when that which sustains them is no more.
Only death is the predictable,
which from birth, hangs about like a shadow,
and neither rich nor poor, white or black,
man or beast, nor any living soul,
can avert the sickle's arc when it swings.

Last Words

In the end was the word,
Simple, crisp, ascetic word;
Not circuitous, not embellished,
Not calligraphic, not polished;
The Word, to death, in defiance,
Faultless, unfaltering in compliance.
Confidently, the word floated,
Smooth, as of oil on Aaron's beard,
Fluently, from the lips of one
Obeyed by sea, by earth, by sun.
And Mary, John and others wept,
Fearing the guard, their distance kept;
The soldier posted near the cross,
Awestruck, he too, for words was lost.
All of creation, pausing, heard,
Angels chanted in one accord:
The Father's mission being accomplished,
The Son, reposing, sighed, "It is finished!"

Blessing

Pax tecum—
not your ancestral or imposed
but its meaning grows
and I bear the fruit of it.
Amid the turmoil and bad blood
the scythe's indiscriminate hacking
the threat of self-extinction
the uncertainty of tomorrow's sun
I bequeath to you the elusive—
Peace!

Glossary

The following are words and expressions, mainly from Kwéyòl, Saint Lucia's second language, that appear in the text:

Page: 16   **Mwen tann ou di ou sé on nonm?** – I hear you say you're a man?

19   **piti kon gwo** – big or small

39   **Soley cho, lapli kwévé** – Sun's shining, it's raining

  Djab ka mayé dèyè kay – The devil is getting married behind the house

41   **djamets** – whores

58   **maléwé** – the poor

  bouillon/bouyon – one pot broth

63   **gajé** – a witch

  soukouyan – vampire, blood sucker

  silans – silence

64   **mové mès** – bad manners

  sin-a-kwa – sign of the cross

69   **tabanka** – the act of being cuckolded

72   **fijé / bèbèl** – wild fruits

73   **mal manman** – effeminate, an effeminate person

74   **kann-kannese** – reference to showy dress style of the 50s/60s

77   **soupsyon** – suspicion

  Polis mouté... – Police climb Morne Gimie / To come and do stupidness

78   **movezté** – wickedness

  An bèl ti plas kon Mòn Gimie – A lovely (little) place like Morne Gimie

81   **sans parole** – without a word spoken

82   *konmès* – mess, nastiness
85   *tèsson* – coalpot
     kanawi – earthen cooking pot
     kawaf – earthen water jar
     kalbas – unensil from tree of the same name
     djapana ….. – medicinal herbs
     sendou – lard
     ti diten etc. – seasonings
     bouyon (bouillon) – broth
95   *kayal* – **a heron**
     mouchoirs – head ties or kerchiefs
     pwalud (Fr. palourde) – **clam**
100 *tout ko-i ka gwaté-i* – she's all itchy
113 *copain-copine* – friends, buddies, mates, associates
     anba tab-ism – bribery, shady deals
     découché – stale, repeated ad nauseam
     bwiyé – local folk dance
115 *makoumè* (malmanman**)** – effeminate
     maco – voyeur

Modeste Downes was born in St. Lucia and grew up in Vieux Fort where he acquired his early education. He taught there for sometime at both the primary and secondary school levels. He has studied at several Caribbean and European institutions thereby gaining insights into the cultures of various peoples.

Besides teaching, the poet has been a cultural, social and political activist, a trade unionist, song writer, book reviewer, a regular contributor to the nation's newspapers, and in 2018 he founded the Cohen & Bruce Williams Literary Award for students. In 1988 he was recognized by the National Youth Council for his outstanding contribution to the work of the Council and the Youth of St. Lucia.

Downes retired as a trade unionist in 2013. He has one daughter and one granddaughter and lives in Saint Lucia.

Critics have placed Modeste Downes in the top echelon of St. Lucian poets. In 2004 he was awarded the George Odlum Award for creative artists. **Phases,** his debut poetry collection, was the winner of the 2005 M&C main prize for literature, and his second collection, **Theatre of the Mind**, was the winner of the 2013 CDF National Arts Award for poetry. In 2015 he was honored with the St. Lucia Laureate's Chair.